DOCTOR TOOTSIE
A YOUNG GIRL'S DREAM

SUZANNE B. KNOEBEL, M.D.

©2003 by Suzanne B. Knoebel, M.D.

Alexie Books
A Division of Alexie Enterprises, Inc.
P.O. Box 3843
Carmel, Indiana 46082

ISBN 09676-416-1-X

Library of Congress
Catalog Card Number
2003092476

Cover art and illustrations by Steven Armour
Cover and text designed by Sara K. Sparks
Interior artwork by Tom Kennard

Printed and bound in the United States of America

Dedicated to
the two men who encouraged me
to be a doctor—
my father and my grandfather.

With all my love and thanks for teaching me so much
And for loving me without qualification.

And with my sincere thanks to Terri B. Kennedy
for her skilled preparation and editing of the manuscript.

PREFACE

This is a story of farm life as a precious inheritance for all men and women physicians. Farm life allows the observance of life in all of its phases and perfects the art of observation and cultivation of reasoning so as to know the true from the false, a vital skill of the good physician.

An inheritance is often thought of as money or goods. More important inheritances are values: honesty, responsibility, consistency, love for love's sake, self-reliance, patience, hard work and sensitivity to the unspoken needs of others. The farm is the best place of all to learn these values and, in the case of physicians, gives a sense of belonging to and understanding something bigger than self. Being a doctor gives purpose to one's life.

SPRING

Chapter One

Nearly every time I asked Mother a question about the farm animals, or whatever, her answer would be, "Now that's a real interesting story!" And she would get all wound up. It didn't take me long to learn how to get some rest from the work of the day, work that somehow seems never-ending on the farm. Mom usually continued with cooking, crocheting or hooking rugs while she talked, but I got to sit and listen. She normally didn't like to see me idle because "idleness was the work of the Devil." But she seemed to accept that listening wasn't being idle. Good listening requires paying attention.

Another of Mom's sayings was, "Pay attention now!"

Gypsy, the German Shepherd, lying by Mom's rocking chair in the late March, sun-warmed library where an afghan was taking shape row by row, stretched her front legs to help pull herself upright. Her tail began to wag.

Mom said matter-of-factly, "Careful, Gypsy, that tail is a lethal weapon."

Gypsy looked up at her as if to say, "I hear you. I'll be careful," and her tail slowed down, losing its whipping action. Even for Gypsy, Mom was a force to be reckoned with.

Mom had a stern exterior. Dark, straight auburn hair pulled back into a bun, a below mid-calf, nondescript, cotton dress partially covered with a bibbed apron, and well-worn house slippers completed the earthy look. Her silk stockings, a holdover from her previous city life, had runners in them. She didn't much care about what she wore.

She put the afghan down. "Your Grandpa must be coming. Quick!

Go set the table! Then Gramp will think dinner is in progress and he'll go sit down and read the paper. If not, he'll prowl around asking what's for dinner and be a general nuisance."

"How do you know Gramp is coming?" I asked as I got out of my chair, hiding at the same time the book I had in my lap. Mom didn't like me to read in the daytime when there was work to be done. She probably wouldn't have approved of this particular book, *The Short History of Medicine*. She would have assumed it had stuff in it that I shouldn't be reading.

"I know that Gramp is coming by what Gypsy does. See her ears perk up? I think she recognizes the sound of his car coming down the hill. To her that sound is synonymous with Gramp. Who else has a car that rattles like his?"

Sure enough, the ancient Ford Model T turned into the driveway. Gramp insisted it was a great car, one which he was going to drive until it or he could go no more, whichever came first. Gypsy pushed open the screen door to meet him. It was a joyous meeting. They loved each other—this man and that dog. They started to play their brand of catch. Gramp would throw the rubber ball he carried in his car to Gypsy, and she would bring it back to him. He would throw it again, each time higher and higher, so she would have to jump higher and higher. When she got tired, she would bring the ball back, lie down in front of him and look up at her master adoringly. It was always the same game.

Mother and I hurried to the kitchen—she to start heating the stew and I, as ordered, to set the table. The biscuits in the oven already were giving off a delicious aroma in the kitchen, a large room with an oak table and chairs where we ate most of our meals. The kitchen extended the entire width of the rear of the house. The windows on the east end looked out over the driveway and allowed the morning sun to brighten the start of each day. After the driveway passed the kitchen, it curved to go to the barn. The west window above the sink allowed a view of the garden and a willow-lined creek just beyond. A stepping-stone walk led to an opening in the willows and the view beyond of a wooden bridge crossing the creek with a cornfield beyond that. The only thing marring part of the beautiful west view from the kitchen was, in my opinion, the clothesline. Mom insisted on drying practically everything outside on wash day. The flapping sheets were like a ghost ballet.

The oak floors of the kitchen shone from daily polishing and monthly waxing. Hooked rag rugs protected the floor in front of the stove and sink. This noon cherry pies just out of the oven were cooling on a wooden cutting board on top of the oven.

As we scrambled around the kitchen, I tried for a continuation of the Gypsy story. "Where did Gypsy come from, Mom?"

"Now that's an interesting story! According to Gramp, she just came walking up the driveway at the home place a year or so ago. She looked so down-and-out, with a hang-dog expression, that Gramp gave her some table scraps and milk. He said she wolfed them down, sighed and went to sleep. Gramp decided she must have been let out down the road. Feeding a big dog like Gypsy costs more than some families can bear. Or, maybe her family moved and left her to fend for herself. He kept her. When Gram passed away, Gramp asked if we could take her. He didn't want to leave her alone so much since he moved around a lot following his horses during racing season."

"How come we can afford her?" I asked.

"She doesn't cost us much. We don't buy most of our food like town folks do. We raise it and she eats what we eat. She doesn't like dog food. Must have been raised that way. She thinks she's a human. We do give her dog biscuits and meaty bones, though, to clean her teeth.

"The farm gives us self-sufficiency. Nearly everything we eat," she waved her right arm in a circle indicating the table, "with the exception of salt and pepper. Everything else comes from the farm—the stew meat, the vegetables, the flour for bread and biscuits, the butter (which you usually churn), the bread-and-butter pickles, the cherries for the pie, the lard for the pie crusts, the milk. Self-sufficiency is an important virtue. Only ask for help when you absolutely can't handle something yourself. It's the farmer's code. Don't be indebted to anyone."

Gramp and Gypsy walked through the kitchen door. "Is that right?

You're indebted to me for talking my son into moving you to the farm."

Mom nodded. "You're right, of course. But like I said only ask for help when you can't handle something yourself. I couldn't handle city life."

I piped up, looking for another story, "What's wrong with city life?"

"Never mind. Gramp is hungry and your dad will be along pretty soon. You ask too many questions. Go ring the dinner bell to call Mr. Alexander and Dodd to dinner. They've worked hard all day in the fields. They'll be hungry."

I glanced through the open door towards my book on the chair. *The Short History of Medicine* would have to wait.

❊ ❊ ❊ ❊ ❊ ❊ ❊ ❊

Gramp, a tall, six-foot-two-inch, still handsome, slightly stooped, white-haired man, had come to live with us after Gram had died, though he still spent some time at the home place where he had grown up and his son after him, my dad.

I adored Gramp. He always had enough time for me and talked to me like grown-ups talk to each other, even though I was only a kid. And there weren't boy and girl jobs in Gramp's opinion. Physical strength was the only thing that made certain things not possible for a girl; still, I got to try them to prove that to myself.

This day Gramp picked me up and twirled me around with Gypsy running in a circle around him.

"Hi, Tootsie. How about going to the track tomorrow? It's time to start the bay colt's training. I'll show you how patience pays off—not that you have any of that yet."

"Oh, Lou, do you think it's safe?" Mom had this thing about race horses. They were notoriously high strung.

"If I didn't, I wouldn't take her." Gramp planted a kiss on Mom's nose. She impatiently brushed him away and turned back to stirring the stew.

During spring, summer and fall Gramp would take me to the family-owned track once or twice a month. Patience he had. He was never too busy to catch a horse for me to ride, never mind that it was a race horse and not a nice, gentle riding academy horse. I usually had to bridle and saddle the beast myself. Gramp would say, "I caught her. You do the rest!" I would walk the calmer horses to dry them off after their post racing or training bath. We called it hot-walking. I would get a nickel for every horse I hot-walked. We didn't have an automatic walker like those I'd seen at the big race tracks. Gramp wouldn't use them. He thought horses benefited from bonding with the humans who talked to them while they were walking. He always said horses were smarter and calmer if they were hand hot-walked. It was good for the human, as well, to stroll with them under the shade of the oak trees that lined the packed dirt walking circle just outside barn doors, which slid on metal tracks so as to open practically the whole side of the barn. When the doors were open, horses that were being groomed in the aisle could see outside and the people grooming them or readying them for training could see anyone or anything passing by. It kept horses and humans in close communion.

Mom, who would have preferred that I stay home and learn how to crochet, reluctantly gave her okay early the next morning for my participation in the beginning training of Peter Nutbert, the bay colt. We left for the track.

Gramp called to me, "Okay, Tootsie," (he always called me Tootsie); "it's time to get moving. The interurban won't wait for us."

The interurban ran from Cranefield to a little village south of Crosston close to the family track, and it was there we got off. I never knew where the interurban went from there. It wasn't a regular station, but the conductor always stopped the little streetcar train when he saw that Gramp and I were on board. Gramp usually had some fresh vegetables or a pie to give him from Mom's garden or kitchen. On this day it was one of the cherry pies from the day before.

The conductor would doff his cap, "Thank the Missus. We sure enjoy her stuff." All women were "Missus" to the conductor. "See you later."

The track to me was the best place in the whole world. The minute we turned in the white painted gate, a flood of peace and belonging washed over me. I felt welcomed, loved and appreciated. Gramp said, "When we get close to the track your nose always begins twitching, just like a horse's, Tootsie." Gramp would wiggle his nose, mimicking my twitching. It made me giggle.

The track encircled three small, natural spring-fed ponds, the largest one of which had an icehouse. Here ice that had been cut from the ponds in the winter was stored with piles of sawdust to keep it from melting. Chunks were chipped off to use in the icebox in the horse barn to store soft drinks for the horsemen. If the refrigerator in the house stopped working, we still had ice for an old icebox in the basement at home.

The ponds were good for fishing. Bluegills, perch and catfish were the predominant inhabitants. Ducks and geese lived there, too. Gramp stocked the ponds once or twice with bass, but bass attacked the other fish, so Gramp stopped putting them in. The horses in the pastures around the ponds used the ponds for drinking, which helped. Because of those ponds, we didn't have to carry water to the horses, except to the pastures where there was no pond access. Those pastures had large tubs filled with water pumped by hand from nearby wells by little girls like me. In fact, that often was my first job when I got off the interurban. And so it was this day, too.

Gramp leaned on the fence surrounding the entrance to the icehouse watching me, smiling and finally saying, "Okay, Tootsie, let's start teaching Peter about his world and his responsibilities."

Walking to the barn I asked, "Gramp, why is Peter so mean that I can't go into his stall?"

"He's not mean. Horses aren't mean unless they have been abused when growing up. He just doesn't know you well enough yet. He doesn't know whether he can trust you or not. He's also a little claustrophobic. He feels trapped in the stall. He wants to get out in the pasture and run. He might knock you over trying to get out of the stall when you open the door. He'll get better when he gets a little older and wiser. But for

right now, just say hello to him when you pass his door and pat his nose if he puts it up against the screen. He'll learn to trust you. Just be patient. He'll get better after he's had a little time to think about it. Incidentally, when a horse is truly mean or mad his eyes will show red. Remember that and don't fool with him or her. Are you ready to ride with me in the training cart?'

"Sure, Gramp."

"Okay. Just watch me get him ready but don't stand too close yet. Horses' eyes are placed on the sides of their head, so they can see not only things directly in front of them but also on either side and behind them and, to some extent, above and below them, a little like a side view mirror in a car.

"Also, unlike humans, horses' eyes aren't set deep in the skull. Bulging out as they do, they have a much wider range of view, so never make a sudden move. That might frighten him even though you're standing directly behind him or some distance away.

"I'll show you and you'll see why he's skittish sometimes. Hold up a finger directly in front of you then close one eye and look at the finger with the other. Then switch eyes. Open the one that is closed and keep looking at the finger. You will notice that the finger appears to jump rapidly an inch or so from one side to the other. With horses' wide-set eyes, it is exaggerated. Suppose Peter sees something with his left eye, but as he draws closer, the right eye catches a view of it. The object appears to move a foot or two. He thinks it's alive.

"Ancestrally, he has been taught to escape predatory animals and they move! Still want to ride with Peter and me?"

"Yeah, I'm not scared." I straightened my shoulders and hooked my thumbs in the waistband of my jeans, trying to look like a cowboy, and headed for the training cart.

The colt we were training, Peter Nutbert, was a colt Gramp said was going to be a champion trotter, win lots of money racing and earn even more as a sire. His pedigree was top of the line, tracing back to the great horse Bret Hanover.

The training cart was the best place to learn everything an eight-year-old, spoiled (so my mother told me) girl needed to know. The rest of my education, my parents said, would come from living on the farm, close to nature and horses, cows, sheep, goats, pigs, chickens, turkeys, ducks, quail, pheasants and pigeons to rub off the perceptions I had

been exposed to in my earlier first years in the city—that money, servants and fancy clothes and cars were the essence of a good life.

The training cart was a heavy oak box-like cart with large wheels and long shafts extending almost to the horse's shoulder. There was an extension behind the horse to prevent him from rearing and coming over backward. Also there was a brake on each wheel to better control him if he tried to bolt. There was room in the cart for two people, particularly if one was a young girl.

"Are we going out on the track, Gramp?"

"No, we're taking the country roads so Peter can learn about cars and motorcycles, other horses in the pastures next to the road and strange sounds and bridges."

We took the cart a short way down the road, where a ditch separated the road from the fences that enclosed the farm fields. It rode smoothly with only an occasional bump. I was asking Gramp about our family—the family that my mother seemed to think was so superior—when Peter shied from a piece of paper along the road side. Gramp had to calm him down, tightening the reins a little and saying, "That's all right, boy. Just a piece of paper."

"Seems like Peter is just looking for things to shy at—just to get our attention," I said.

"No," Gramp laughed, "he's just a young horse protecting himself. Remember what I told you about horses' eyes? Besides, he's just having a little fun. He's bored."

"You think he thinks about that?"

"Sure he does. Watch when I say, 'Peter, are you okay? Do you want to go a little faster?'"

Sure enough Peter's ears flipped backwards towards us as if to hear us better and increased his speed to signal his understanding and pleasure.

"Maybe we'll tell him a story. You asked about our family. He'll like that one. You come from a highly respected English family, the records for which go back to about the sixteenth century. The men were considered to be landed gentry, entitled to have a coat of arms, but weren't royalty. Basically they were farmers. Land was their cherished possession and medicine was their contribution to others. This runs deep in your heritage.

"The first family members in this country came to Jamestown in approximately 1660. One of them, who became prominent in the civic affairs of the colony, was a member of the governing body and the clerk of one county. He was rewarded for his efforts toward the well-being of his community by being deeded thousands of acres of land in what was to become parts of Kentucky, Ohio and Indiana. His land rights were extensive, maybe including some of which you, Peter and I are now riding on. The Miami Indians still lived on this land, of course, but our ancestors dealt and traded with them.

"John, that was his name, was a medicine man also. As a matter of fact, most all of your ancestors were physicians—except me. I'm the black sheep. But being on the farm is good training for a future doctor like you." Peter was sprinting along smartly, seeming to enjoy himself.

"I'm going to be a doctor?"

"Yes, your father grew up on this farm and he's the best doctor around. He always says that a farm background is good training for a doctor. He says you're going to follow in his footsteps. You're independent enough that you wouldn't like a work-for-others career. Individualism runs in doctors. It has to. They have to trust themselves."

"How can I be a doctor with a name like Tootsie? And I've always wanted to be a doctor *and* a farmer."

"You can combine the two like your dad and your ancestors. You had two great grandpas who were frontier doctors." He smiled, "Gentle girl farmer and doctor. Maybe we had better start calling you by your real name, Stephanie. That way, you'll get accustomed to it."

"Never mind. I like Doctor Tootsie better. Mom says that you're poor, Gramp, and I shouldn't ask you for anything."

Gramp laughed. "I may not have any coins in my pocket but I'm one of the wealthiest men around, Doctor Tootsie. I've got you, Peter and all of this land. What more could a man want?"

He hugged me as we turned into the stable area. "Your mother overdoes this money bit. Probably trying to send you a 'money isn't everything' message."

Peter was now sweating rather heavily and Gramp turned him toward the barn. "He's had enough for today. Needs a bath."

"Can I hot-walk him to dry him off after his bath, Gramp?"

"Not yet, Doc. We'll let his groom, Hank, walk him. Hank and Peter are friends now and Hank talks to him while they're walking. It relaxes both of them."

After Peter was handed over to Hank, Gramp patted Peter's neck saying, "Good boy." Gramp and I had our usual lunch at the track: canned peaches, cheese and crackers. Later in the summer we would substitute tomatoes from the garden for the peaches.

After lunch it was horse and people rest time. For Gramp it was a nap. For me it was back to my book. I was reading about Hippocrates, the Father of Medicine. During his time, Greek medicine reached its zenith. In fact, the book said medicine itself reached a height not attained again for 500 years. It became in his hands an art, a science and a profession. I could do that! I knew I could.

Gramp didn't tolerate cowardice from anyone, including me. In mid-afternoon, after his nap, he decided he wanted to move one of his older mares, Princess, to a new pasture. The problem for me was that she was blind from an old eye infection and was nervous when she didn't know where she was or where she was going. Gramp put a lead strap on her halter and asked me to lead her to the new field. He would follow me in the track car, a Plymouth coupe with a rumble seat. It rattled almost as much as his Model T. Princess didn't like this arrangement and started to prance and rear. I was afraid she would step on me or break loose from my grip. I called to Gramp, "I'm scared, Gramp. Princess is scared, too."

He said, "Okay, I'll lead her. You drive the car." That was even scarier. He saw my hesitation and said, "Try singing to her. If that doesn't work we'll shift jobs."

I started to sing *The Star Spangled Banner* and sure enough she settled down. It distracted her. It distracted me, too, as I concentrated on that hard-to-sing national anthem.

Sometimes Mom would let us stay all night at the track. We slept in the feed barn, a cool, red brick building full of sacks, barrels and harnesses in various stages of repair. The problem was that there were always scuffling sounds, but I was too happy and tired to care. I never asked what critters were making the noise. I didn't want to know. I was sure it was mice or, even worse, rats. But the smell of hay and leather reminded me of where I was and made me feel at peace.

Tonight, though, we took the interurban back to Cranefield. To-

Welcome to Hamilton North PL - Atlanta Branch
You have the following items:

1. Dr. Tootsie : a young girl's dream
   Barcode: 78294000280623
   Due: 2021-11-16 23:59

✓ ②. Dearest Dorothy, slow down, you're wearing us out!
   Barcode: 78294000184800
   Due: 2021-11-16 23:59

3. Letters of a woman homesteader
   Barcode: 78294000159407
   Due: 2021-11-16 23:59

HMNTH-ATL 2021-10-25 17:10
You were helped by MARY

morrow was plowing time and I wanted to follow behind the plow looking for arrowheads.

On the ride home, I asked Gramp why Dad had moved Mom to the farm. He said, "She'll tell you if she wants to. Don't pester her about it."

When we got home, it was just in time for leftovers from an earlier supper that Mom, Dad and the Alexanders had shared. I was informing Mom that Gramp told me I was going to be a doctor and how happy I was about it.

Her response was, "Oh, for heaven's sake, what next? Why can't you be like other little girls? Grow up, get married and live your life taking care of your family? Oh, well, you won't get into medical school anyway and even if you do, you won't last. You're too spoiled. You want everything your way."

My face fell. I'd have to think about that!

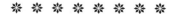

Dear Diary:

What a great day! I spent all day with Gramp training Peter and learning all about horses' eyes and the history of our family. I still don't know why we live on a farm though. Gramp told me I shouldn't ask. He taught me about the power of kindness and paying attention to the unspoken needs of others—animals and humans alike. I will remember that a pat on the shoulder is worth a lot of words. It silently links the patter and the pattee. That's the way Gramp relates to Peter anyway.

Gramp also told me that I could be a doctor. Mom didn't agree. She said that even if I got into medical school, which was unlikely because the male-controlled profession didn't want girls taking up their precious seats in medical school, I wouldn't last. I don't understand that. But I'm beginning to wonder whether she's right. The Short History of Medicine book I'm reading is fascinating. It should be made into a movie. It's pretty hard on women doctors though. Some of them were thought to be witches and were burned at the stake. Pretty scary!

I'll have to talk to Dad about all of this.

Chapter Two

Plowing was really tough work. When the farmer had to turn over the ground, the pull required of the horses and ploughman was tremendous. Farm horses, or draft horses as they were called, were heavily muscled animals with strong bones and big feet, but they were truly gentle, willing giants. One time I remembered Bell, one of the strongest horses, had been asked to pull some large logs from the mud of the creek that ran through the farm. She tried so hard that she fell to her knees until Mom told the men, "That's enough. Poor Bell. Get some chains and we'll hook them up to the truck even if the fenders get pulled off. I don't care. Bell's done her best and that's all anyone—horse or human—should be expected to do."

During one of our interurban rides, I asked Gramp why we didn't have a tractor and big plow like I saw on most of the farms along the way when we were training Peter.

"That requires a rather complicated answer," he had said looking very thoughtful. "But I'll give it a try."

"First of all, to justify expensive equipment, you need to be into big business farming that would require many workers. Even if you could find the workers, it would be more expensive than buying the equipment. Most of the farms you see around us are big farms and selling their products is the way they make their living. While we have more land than we farm, much of it is used for other purposes such as wild life preservation. That's by your dad's choice.

"Secondly," he went on, "depending on equipment results in losing your self-reliance. Equipment always needs repair of some kind and if you can't do it yourself, you have to depend on others to do it.

"Thirdly, your dad and I are old-fashioned. We like to preserve some of the old ways just so little girls will ask questions."

"Just like doctors. They always ask questions," I smarted off.

He gave me a hug, saying, "Yes they do. And that's enough for today. I know your dad has been thinking about buying Mr. Hendricks' farm that adjoins the one where you live. If that happens, it will require some modern equipment to farm it."

Our hired man, Mr. Alexander, was already in the field when I got there the next morning. He could hardly stop laughing when he looked over his shoulder and saw this skinny kid in overalls (me) with blonde hair pulled back in a ponytail walking behind him and the plow looking down intently at the soil that the plow turned over. He was a powerfully-built, middle-aged man, his biceps of amazing size, his face darkly tanned even though he wore a straw cap to protect his early-balding scalp. He had come to work on the farm to pay off his doctor's bill. He stayed on with Dad and Mom as hired help when his debt was paid. His wife helped Mom in the kitchen and with the housekeeping chores. They lived in a little cement block cottage a short distance from the main house. They ate with us as part of the family.

When Mr. Alexander stopped to give the horses a rest and himself a drink of lemonade that Mom had delivered, he asked, "What are you doing, Doc? Looking for worms to go fishing with?" He had learned to call me Doc from Gramp.

Using my most sophisticated voice, I said, "Ugh. I use artificial bait, Mr. Alexander. How you guys can thread a squiggly worm on a hook is beyond me. No, no worms. I'm looking for arrowheads. These fields are full of them, Gramp says. He has a little bag full of them which he has found around here. They're easier to see in fresh dirt. If the dirt dries out, the arrowheads and dirt become the same color and the arrowheads are hard to see." We both looked up at the trees above us, appreciating their shade.

"I hadn't thought of that, but should have," Mr. Alexander shook his head. "I'm one-half Indian myself."

"You are?" I looked at him with more respect from then on. I was fascinated by Indians and Indian folklore.

Bell and Jim, the horses assigned to plowing that day, were dozing, near the trees, while we talked, an occasional flipping of the tail to brush off an annoying fly as their only activity.

Mr. Alexander sat down next to me. "The Miami Indian village of Kekionga was near where the St. Mary and St. Joseph Rivers join to form the Maumee. That area is now called Ft. Wayne. There were some fierce fights in the area before things got portioned off between the French and the English traders, eventually becoming a territory of the United States. Course, some of the arrowheads were used for things other than fighting like getting dinner, rabbits primarily, and a few deer."

I looked up and saw Mom coming down the lane next to the field. "Whoops, here comes Mom again. We'd better get movin', Mr. Alexander, or she'll make us plow until midnight."

"Yes. You're right. Let's go. Good hunting."

But there were no arrowheads that day so I headed for the house. As I waved goodbye to Mr. Alexander, I could hear him telling Jim while slapping his rear with the reigns, "Get up there and pull your weight. You're making Bell do all of the work." Jim was a little lazy and

Little Turtle of the Miamis

had to be reminded fairly often of his role. Dolly, our third draft horse, was the best of the three of them. She liked to work alone and was Mr. Alexander's choice for special work that required some smarts.

Mr. Alexander was originally from Oklahoma. He rode the rails out of Oklahoma to Chicago during the dust bowl days, then worked his way to the Cranefield area stopping there when he got a severe lung infection, probably the result of riding the rails. He told great stories about himself and his fellow "tramps" dodging the railroad cops. Another benefit from having Mr. Alexander (I never called him by his first name as it wasn't considered appropriate for kids to call grown-ups by their first names) living on the farm was that his brother, Dodd, often visited him from Oklahoma. Dodd was quite a yodeler. When the milking was done and all the farm animals bedded down for the night, he would sit on the porch with us and yodel while we watched the lightning bugs turn their lights on and off, seemingly in synchrony with each other.

It was almost dinnertime. Dinner was at noon on the farm, because the men had to have energy for the rest of the day as well as have a break. So did the horses.

We all ate together around the large oak kitchen table—Mr. and Mrs. Alexander, Gramp, Dad, Mom, and me. The conversation was mostly about farm matters.

Gramp always said that Mom planted her garden too soon, because when she didn't wait until after the torrential spring rains or the last frost, she often had to replant. But she could hardly wait. After all of the hard spring work was done, seeing the first green sprouts of corn and soybeans, leaf lettuce, green onions, radishes and the greening of the trees and lilac bushes, the work part was forgotten. An apple orchard lined our driveway, and it became a cloud of blooms that was awe-inspiring. Soon there would be transparent apples that made great applesauce, apple pies and sour eating apples, delicious with a little salt on them.

This spring Gramp was right. The rains had ruined some of Mom's neat rows in her garden at the west side of the house. It was really a small field, bigger than most gardens. Mom raised strawberries (a lot of picking to be done later on), sweet corn, watermelons, cantaloupes, lima beans, peas, turnips, lettuce, cabbage, zucchini, cucumbers, radishes, green onions, squash, green beans and other vegetables. This spring she'd asked me to help plant the radishes. I guess she thought I knew how. But I didn't. I planted the tiny little seeds so close together that they came up "thick as hair on a dog's back" Mom said. I had to pull out what seemed to be hundreds of little plants so the others could survive. Everything needs living room. She never asked me to help with seed planting again.

I did plant potatoes. First, though, you had to cut the potatoes so that each half or quarter of the seed potato had an "eye" or germination site, but only one. I would talk to the cats about all kinds of things while sitting on the back porch "eyeing" potatoes. The cats came to the house from the barn when they saw someone sitting on the porch. They liked human company.

Dad came home early one day the next week and joined the cats, sitting on the porch step just below me.

As I continued to eye potatoes, I told him about Mom telling me I'd never last in medical school even if I got in. "Why does she think that, Dad?"

Dad got a thoughtful look on his face, his eyes narrowing a little. A frown developed. "I'm not sure, Steph. Perhaps she saw all the stuff women medical students had to put up with when she was a nurse. The male students took delight in teasing the women students and were even more delighted when the girls took them seriously. This egged them on.

"The girls who didn't have a hard time in medical school didn't overreact to the guys' teasing. They just smiled and if they said anything it was something like, 'You're funny. Keep it up.' They were the ones who didn't try to act like the guys. They were just themselves.

"Just remember if you're good in what you do, let the others try to be as good as you. Don't lower yourself to their level. But don't let them know that you think you're better than they are. Don't have a chip on your shoulder or they will try to knock it off. You know Dr. Kirby? She was in my class in med school. We all wanted to study with her. She had a way to make us understand concepts. She was number one in her class. Talk to her sometime when you see her while you're waiting for me in the hospital."

"Dad, I read in the book you loaned me, *The Short History of Medicine*, about Hippocrates being called the Father of Medicine. Gosh! He was born 400 years before Christ. The book said that doctors still take the Hippocratic oath when they graduate from medical school. Did you take it?"

"Yes, I did. And I'm proud of it! I think of it more frequently than you might imagine. It states rules for moral behavior. To heal the sick has been the challenge and the obligation of the physician throughout the ages and to transmit knowledge to other physicians."

The next steps in preparing the fields for planting were disking and harrowing. That involved breaking up the clods created by the plowing and smoothing out the surface. Of course, those processes broke up arrowheads, too, so I lost my enthusiasm for that aspect of tilling the land.

After the plowing, disking and harrowing came the planting. Planting in straight lines was the challenge. Bell and Jim had been doing it so long they somehow knew to stay straight. Fields were more beautiful with straight, long rows of budding soybeans and corn. Some farmers broadcast the seeds by throwing them out by hand with wide sweeps of their arms. That was too untidy and slow for Mom. She and I did it only in areas too small for mechanical planters and even then we had to be very careful not to cultivate too close to the fence rows because Dad didn't want to destroy the natural bird habitats that wild fence rows provided. Wild fence rows were thought by many to be the sign of a lazy farmer. Dad didn't care what they thought. He thought more about the quail and pheasants that the fence rows would protect spring, summer, fall and winter.

It became a family joke when Mr. Alexander would ask Dad if he wanted him to clean out the fence rows. We all waited to watch Dad's feigned mean-looking face and hear his explosive, "No, damn it!" That always ended the fence row conversation until the next time. Dad was one of the early environmentalists and we got the message. Even Mom, who really liked neat fence rows, had given up trying to change Dad— on that score at least. Dad often told us that clean fence rows were destroying our farmland, allowing the wind to sweep off the topsoil. "We would pay for neatness some day," he predicted.

Mr. Alexander was a land conservationist, too. One rainy day while we were working in the barn, Mr. Alexander was making repairs and building birdhouses, one of his favorite pastimes while I watched. I asked, "Mr. Alexander, I read once that Indians were land worshippers. What does that mean? Like Dad's fence rows?"

"Well, not exactly, Tootsie. But along the same lines. The Indians believed that we must not destroy our lands, for when we start destroying our environment we begin to destroy ourselves. The Indian belief is that life comes from the earth. We don't give the earth its life, it gives life to us. It is the Indian religion."

"Dad is committed to the land in a way. Is that what you mean?"

"Yes. I think it goes with being a doctor. Men and women who choose to be doctors must make a total commitment to their profession and pay a high price in self-denial. Commitment is their religion, as it should be according to Indian teaching."

"Gramp told me that all of our ancestors except for him were doctors."

Mr. Alexander smiled. "You'd better listen to him, Tootsie, and to nature."

"Tell me about Indian medicine men and women—if there were any women."

Mr. Alexander kept working on a birdhouse he was building. There were bird houses all over. "Well, Medicine Men were believed to have been chosen by the gods and were powerful personages. The women were herbalists and helped with the birth of children."

It was getting too hard for me to follow so I said, "Thanks, Mr. Alexander. I'll see you later. Will you tell me more Indian stuff when I get back?"

"Sure. We'll talk some more."

Dear Diary:

What an exciting day! I learned that Mr. Alexander is one-half Indian and he promised to tell me more. He must have told Dad about my interest in Indian lore because Dad brought me a book from the library about Indian medicine. It talks about the commitment Indian doctors must have to serve their band and the land. Honesty, too, is a requirement for medicine men and women. Don't deal in false hopes or, for that matter, dire predictions not based in fact, was the message I got. Dad also told me about women doctors—the ones who were accepted by nearly all of the men. Even those dumb boys (he called them that, I didn't) know when the other team has won (the women doctors). The women in medicine won, he believes, by their attitude that doctors are doctors—not men-doctors or women-doctors. So the man-woman arguments were downplayed. He also believed that the history of women in medicine, as with men, is intertwined with their daily lives, religious beliefs, social customs and economic issues. All of these have changed throughout the ages as has the acceptance of women as physicians. For example, he said that during colonial days in this country most health care was delivered by women in the home. Then when more and more men were trained in Europe and came back to America with new ideas and instruments, they ran into women caregivers. The male doctors began their campaigns against females in medicine. They said that women's moral qualities and social qualities should make them remain as masters of their "life sphere" home. Poppycock!

CHAPTER THREE

One day that spring Mom called me frantically. I was walking from the barn to the house. She was outside standing on the well platform. When I got there she pointed at a snake which was in the process of swallowing a frog. "Do something," Mom said. "The frog looks so scared."

I didn't know what to do but I picked up the snake by its tail and dropped it on the cement well platform. In the process the frog dropped out of the snake's mouth. The snake then turned toward a kitten which was watching the show, struck it and in just a minute or two the kitten died. Just then Gramp arrived on the scene and killed the snake with a hoe he was carrying. "Don't touch that snake. It's a copperhead and very poisonous."

When I told him I had already picked it up he said, "Oh, my God!" grabbed me by the hand and took me to the house to read about snakes in the encyclopedia. Every moment on the farm instructs mostly about the beauties of nature, but nature also can be cruel. Those times are lessons, too. It said in the book Dad brought me that the Indians taught their children which plants were blessed and which were cursed and to be avoided.

As I stared out over the pasture trying to forget the snake episode, I saw Ginger, my pinto pony, with her new baby standing beside her. Ginger had done the whole birthing herself and now she was quietly grazing, occasionally turning to nudge her baby to her bag to make sure she had a nourishing meal.

I called to Mom and Gramp, "Look, Ginger had her baby all by herself! Isn't she beautiful?"

Gramp assured me that she was a true beauty, chestnut with white pinto markings and a white blaze down her face. "Why don't we call her Twylah for the granddaughter of a great Seneca Indian Medicine Man?

She will be wise and loving."

"That's great, Gramp. Thanks." I hurried down to the pasture to get a closer look. Ginger moved so she was always between her new charge and me. She was going to be a good mother.

It wasn't long after Twylah's birth that the other new spring babies began to arrive. Spring was here for sure and new baby lambs, piglets, fuzzy little chicks and ducks were hatching daily.

"The whole farm is a maternity ward," Dad said one day at dinner.

All of the new babies and their mothers needed around-the-clock checking. Lambs in particular. I couldn't understand why we had to have lambs so early in the spring, often when it was still cold, particularly at night. Gramp explained it to me. "It is important that they be ready for marketing in the early fall." I didn't like to hear about the marketing part. Anyway, during lambing time, we all took rotations every two hours to go to the barn to see if there were new lambs and if they were up and nursing. If they weren't, or their mothers weren't claiming them, as sometimes happened for reasons no one knew, we would pick the lambs up and take them to the house to get them started.

It was really interesting. The first thing we did was give them about a teaspoonful of whiskey. Their little tails would flip and they would look startled. Then we would have baby bottles filled with goat milk and put the nipple to their mouth, squeezing a little into their mouth first so they could get the taste for things to come. It usually didn't take long for them to start pulling on the rubber nipple. When they were able to stand and nurse enthusiastically, we would put a spot or two of kerosene on their backs so their mothers would accept them. The kerosene made all of the babies smell the same so the mother wasn't able to tell by smell whether or not the little one trying to nurse was really her baby. Mothers were very unaccepting of another ewe's baby, so in our barn all lambs smelled like kerosene and even orphan lambs were accepted by all the ewes. Sometimes we had to keep the weakest lambs in the basement where it was warm all night. I got accustomed to hearing little lambs bleating all night long.

One early morning, very early in fact, when I went to the barn to check on the new arrivals, I saw one of the ewes lying down. She was making sounds like she was having pain and her eyes were dull. Mom was a great believer in eyes as a reflector of a healthy or sick state, and I knew this ewe was very sick. Her eyes said so. There was a bad smell about her.

Dad and Mom were away at a medical convention and Mr. Alexander had taken Gramp to the home place to help him with his garden cultivation.

I didn't know whether the vet would come just on my say, but Dad had always told me that if you don't know what's wrong with a patient, get a consult from someone who might. This ewe was my patient, and I didn't know what was wrong, so I called our veterinarian. The risk of doing nothing was greater than the risk of looking foolish.

I must have sounded desperate because he came right over.

His greeting was, "What's the matter, Doc? This one too tough for you?" The "Doc" nickname had gotten around.

I nodded and led him to the sick ewe. It didn't take him long to diagnose that the lamb inside was dead and the mother was getting infected. He removed the dead lamb and gave the ewe an antibiotic injection saying, "I think she'll be all right in a day or so. I'll come back this evening to check on her."

Stripping off his gloves, he patted me on the shoulder and said, "Good girl."

I responded with, "I'm not a horse, Doctor Winter. That's what I say to Twylah—good girl!"

I heard him laughing all the way to his truck.

✻ ✻ ✻ ✻ ✻ ✻ ✻ ✻

After the lambs were able to fend for themselves and their pre-ferred life was to play with the other young lambs, it was time for the moms to get sheared. Wool was another of Mom's cash crops. Profes-sional sheep shearers traveled around the countryside in their modified house trailers, shearing by appointment. Mostly they did the big flocks first and came to smaller farms when time permitted. So we had to wait patiently.

We would drive the ewes into a small enclosure so the shearer could catch them easily. When they had wrestled the struggling sheep to a standstill, they straddled them and sheared the wool off with bat-tery-powered clippers in strips so it could be rolled up. I would stand by and when a roll was presented to me, I would weigh it, record the ewe's ear tag number so we could identify the best wool producers, and put the rolled-up wool in a sack.

When an ewe was sheared she looked so funny—almost naked. I thought they seemed embarrassed, running around nude. Occasionally, one would get nicked by the clipper and I would have to put some coal tar on the nick so the flies couldn't irritate the site and cause infestations of maggots. They're nasty looking things, little white worms. When Gramp told me that maggots were once used to clean out wounds be-cause of some healing product they made, I almost got sick.

❋ ❋ ❋ ❋ ❋ ❋ ❋ ❋

Calves were different from lambs. Because they were too big to carry to the house, we had to stay in the stall with them and their moth-

ers until all was well. We used buckets of milk, pushing their faces into it until they sneezed. Then we would take each calf over to its mother and give it a taste of her milk. Usually it worked.

Baby chicks were yet another problem. These fuzzy yellow balls had to stay warm under heat lamps in the chicken house until they

31

grew a little and could be turned out into a pen. The trouble was that they all tended to pile up one on top of another under the hood. Suffocation was not a rare event. So somebody—usually me—had to go every hour or so and stir them up. Chickens were a cash crop for Mom during the summer and fall, so in addition to not wanting them to kill each other, we wanted to save as much money as possible.

Chickens were not my favorite farm habitants. They didn't seem to have any sense of self or for anything else for that matter. But because they were easier to feed and water—they had feeders that prevented them from messing up their food with their droppings—they usually fell under my job description. Even when people stopped by to purchase their Sunday dinner, I had to go catch the one they pointed out. I had a long stick with a metal hook at the end that I put around the chicken's legs to keep them from moving so I could catch them. I refused to kill them though. The purchasers had to do that.

Turkeys were a little more intelligent but not much. They required a lot of care, too, as they were subject to several diseases. They too were a cash crop popular around holiday times, so we didn't want them to die, nor did we want to sell sick birds. They had to receive their disease-prevention vaccination shots, just like children. But first we had to catch them. Gramp would drive them in a low wire cage, ten or twelve at a time and send me in to hand them out to him where he waited with a syringe and needle to give them their shots. I hated that job. It was hot and dusty.

In the fall around Thanksgiving and Christmas, Mom would sell cleaned turkeys ready for the oven. It was a hard job for her, but she always said, "Nothing lasts forever. This will be over soon."

Dad and Gramp, being naturalists, raised quails and pheasants so they could be turned out when they were old enough to take care of themselves. Baby quail are no bigger than bumble bees, and if they got out of their pen it was a riot to find them even in short grass. I had to crawl on hands and knees to search for them. Sometimes we never found them. I hated to think that some animal had a bird for lunch.

Since raccoons had to wash their food before eating it, when I wanted to have some fun I'd get some crumbly cornbread from Mom and put it on a rock just outside the wire of the pens. It didn't take the

was hilarious. They'd look around trying to find it in the water and around the rock. I'd watch them for the laughs until Mom said, "No more." And raccoons are so smart they would shuck corn with their little paws so that some of it would fall outside the cage, luring the chickens outside to their death. When a chicken got close enough, the raccoon would reach out and grab it around the neck, bite off its head, wash it in the water bowl and have a chicken head lunch.

Mom was livid and stated her opinion in no uncertain terms. "No more raccoons. They're only good to be coats." We had never heard her say such a thing. And so it was. The raccoons were turned loose.

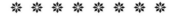

When school was finally out in early June, I became a full time farmer and told Gramp that I wanted to learn how to milk. I, for sure, learned responsibility, Gramp style. "Okay, Tootsie, but remember when you start something you have to finish it. Come to the barn at five

o'clock tonight and I'll pick a cow for you to learn on. One that is patient." I didn't get the implication of that until seven o'clock that night when I was still trying to milk dry Old Jerse, as she was called. Gramp stopped by occasionally to see how I was doing and explained why it was necessary to milk a cow dry. Otherwise, that cow will stop producing. He finally agreed around seven o'clock that he would finish milking her and that I should go have some supper. Perhaps, he said, I should begin my milking career with Nanny the goat. Goats were easier to milk.

I readily agreed only to find out as time went on what a big mistake that was. Nanny refused to let anyone else milk her after I became her friend. Mr. Alexander had made a little box for her to stand on when I milked so I wouldn't have to sit on the ground. He also made a low, three-legged milking stool for me. I sang to Nanny while I milked. She must have liked my singing, because she would doze off.

Nanny's choice of me as her preferred milker ended Gramp's and my overnight stays at the track. We had to come home so I could milk her. That's a responsibility!

Dear Diary:

I guess responsibility is the greatest thing I learned this spring. Responsibility to the new arrivals for their survival and health. And, once they are dependent on you, you don't desert them just because it's inconvenient for you. Once trust has been established don't make them constantly adjust to strangers! I guess that's why Dad doesn't share night call with the other physicians in his building. He believes that on-call doctors don't know his patients as well as he does and, therefore, can't always make appropriate decisions about their care particularly if a problem arises in the middle of the night. When Dad would be gone for a day or so—an unusual event— he would write notes in his patients' charts outlining what to do if, in his absence, something acute came up. Usually he wrote, "Call me wherever I am." Since I had to wait at the hospital while he wrote the notes, my reward would be that he would let me read them. He's starting my doctor training early. I'm learning also that what I read is privileged information to be discussed only with him. I only wish Dad wouldn't come home from night call so tired. Lately he just collapses into bed.

❋ ❋ ❋ ❋ ❋ ❋ ❋ ❋

Usually my diary entry was the last thing I did before going to sleep, but this evening it was different. I couldn't sleep. I was reviewing the events of the day when I was waiting for Dad to write his notes. Dr. Kirby, the lady doctor who had been in Dad's medical school class, stopped by to say hello to me. I must have had a faraway look on my face or something because she said, "Those must be pretty deep thoughts, Tootsie. Got time to tell me about them, girl to girl?"

"Sure, Dr. Kirby, if you have time."

She sat down on the bench, pulling me closer to her. "Certainly I do. Shoot."

"I told Mother that I wanted to be a doctor and she acted like I was some kind of nut. She said being a doctor was too tough for me."

"Don't believe that for a moment, Tootsie. It's hard work, sure, but the learning is exciting, even thrilling. I had more fun in med school and in my internship and residency than I had before or have had since. It's a wonderful world. Doctoring has its sadnesses and its joys, but always its rewards."

"How long will it take me to become a doctor?"

"A long time, sweetie, but you'll be so busy you won't even think about it. You'll be sorry when it's over. First, it's regular college, four years. Then it's med school, another four years, then an internship for one year."

"That's nine years!" I had never thought of it in those terms.

Dr. Kirby smiled, recognizing my sudden reality of the years ahead. "Never mind. As I said, it will be just a phase in your lifetime commitment. You didn't think about grade school and high school being a long time, did you? The next phase will be a three-year residency, followed by a three to five year specialty training, depending if you choose to specialize and in which specialty."

"Wow!" I started to count on my fingers. "That's twelve to fifteen years."

"Just a phase in a whole lifetime, my dear."

Just then Dad walked into the lounge. "What are you two conniving about?"

"Just about preparing Tootsie to become a doctor."

Dad laughed. "That's a while yet. By the time she gets ready to apply, we fellows may be in the minority. It's heading that way. All she will need is good grades, good humor and the willingness to work hard. She already has the last two so the emphasis should be on grades and self-discipline."

Dad put out his hand. "Come on, Tootsie, time to go home. Nanny needs milking."

On the way home I told him of my concerns. "Dad, I haven't seen anything very encouraging for women in *The Short History of Medicine*."

Dad looked at me, "Are you having second thoughts?"

"Maybe a little bit. It's all so confusing."

"Let's see if this helps," Dad cleared his throat as though he was about to give a lecture. "What may make the prospect of becoming a physician worthwhile for young women like yourself is the enrichment of her life, the sense of self-expression which cannot be dismissed even after the attacks of doubt it may bring."

"Thanks, Dad. I can see that farming enriches life and allows self-expression."

On that note, I drifted off to sleep.

SUMMER

Chapter Four

Blessed summer, a reward for all of the spring plowing and planting work, at least for a while until the summer work began. Haymaking and threshing, in particular. Picking garden produce was a special reward.

The best treat of all was that I got to spend more time with Gramp and continue to experience the joys of horse racing. It was harness racing time in the Midwest, and Gramp and I were on the County Fair circuit. We also had our own races at Gramp's track. He didn't want to send Peter to the fairs as yet. He wanted him to be older and more mentally mature before stressing him, so we had "play" races of our own.

My horse in our home races was Emma J. Stone, locally known as a world champion lone pacer. She had won many real races in her time and knew the game. She would limber up on the track for a short distance then turn and gradually accelerate to full racing speed so that when she saw the starting gate pulled to the side she was already racing.

Emma really didn't need a driver. But I held the reigns acting like one. The horse knew what to do. When she had circled the track and passed the finish pole where the groom, Hank, was perched on a lifeguard-like stand, she would look up at him as if to ask, "How was that speed? Okay?" Then she would gradually slow down to a walk at the exit to the barn. By that time, Hank was there to get her, pat her on her shoulder, help me get off the sulky and take Emma to the barn for unharnessing. It was then my turn to give her a sponge bath and lead her around the walking circle until she was dry. I wondered why I always won every race. Emma probably already knew that Gramp was holding his horse back to let her win. His horse was there just to give Emma a little push. She was very competitive and didn't like to be passed.

I once asked Gramp when we were at one of the tracks where

betting was allowed why he never bet. He always seemed to know which horse was going to win. His answer was, "You don't bet on something or someone you love. There should be no link between monetary considerations and love. You don't want to end up blaming someone you love for anything."

As usual, when Gramp made a proclamation like that I didn't ask why anymore for a while.

When the races were over at the fairs, we'd go visit the exhibits. Mom's white coconut cake always won a blue ribbon.

I had to take care of my ducks. They'd already won one blue ribbon—two more to go. They were waddling round and round in their cages, entertaining the kids around the pen who would mimic their waddles and go "quack, quack" at them. If ducks could smile, I thought these ducks certainly were.

We went to the State Fair every year. Mom was particularly interested in the sheep. They were her hobby. She raised registered Suffolks. She always thought hers were as nice as those at the fair, but didn't want

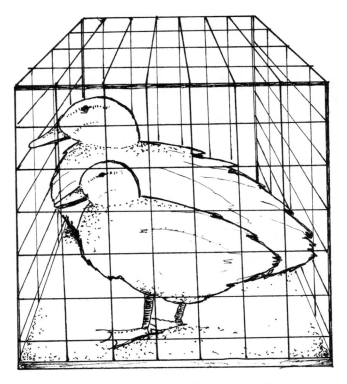

to expose them to the crowds, so she didn't enter them.

One beautiful day when there was a break in fair activities and I was home on the farm, I let Ginger out for some exercise as I wanted to play with Twylah in the barn without causing Ginger any concern or distracting Twylah. Actually, I wasn't playing exactly, I was trying to teach Twylah love and respect so when she was a yearling we could be assured she wouldn't be afraid of being around humans. I wanted to build trust.

She was a beautiful little filly with soft eyes and a sweet disposition already. She loved the attention.

I told her about her name. "You're named after the granddaughter of a great Seneca Indian Medicine Man. That's quite an honor." Twylah seemed to listen with interest. For me this confirmed Gramp's teaching that animals and people could talk to each other if they only listened and observed.

My lessons for her were based on praise and sweet rewards. She dearly loved peppermint candy, so when she did something very well I told her, "you're a good girl" in my softest, most loving voice and gave her a peppermint. If she did something naughty such as trying to bite or kick, I'd scold her saying, "Look at you, acting like a naughty girl"— no sweet reward. She learned good from bad behavior very quickly.

Gramp didn't approve of my rewarding method—sweets. One day when he came to the barn, he happened to arrive during a training session. "Tootsie, I'd like to talk to you about your reward system for Twylah."

"Sure, Gramp. Am I doing something wrong?"

"I think so, Tootsie, and my opinion comes from years of experience. If you reward youngsters with candy, they learn to demand it, associating it with good performance. In the case of horses, they will start nipping your hand and even searching your pockets where the candy usually comes from. And, of course, they search with their mouths. It's a bad habit to encourage."

"I understand what you're saying, Gramp. Twylah already searches my coat pocket. I just thought it was cute. How can I break the pattern?"

"Gradually, just like you have been training her. Start by not giving her candy every time you praise her. Substitute another reward—a soft pat on the neck or a brushing with a soft brush. She'll learn eventually that there are rewards other than candy associated with your sweet talk."

"Okay, Gramp, I'll try it."

"Don't expect instant results. It's like stopping cigarette smoking. Gradual withdrawal is easier than cold turkey stopping. Incidentally, don't smoke! I hope you haven't tried that horrible weed."

"No, Gramp. Can't smoke in barns, you know."

He hugged me and went about the business he came to the barn for—to check a rather bad cut on one of the cow's legs. The cow had caught her leg in a broken fence and, getting panicky, had pulled her leg through the hole tearing a big piece of skin off. Dad called me over for one of his prevention lectures when it happened. "You see why we have to be so careful about keeping the fences in good repair? It might just have been Twylah reaching through for something that looked good to eat." I had just added another job for me. I walked the fences nearly every day in the pastures that the animals used, to check for holes or other fence hazards that might cause injuries to the animals.

Make hay while the sun shines is the theme of farm life in August. Before Dad and Gramp convinced themselves that modern equipment was respectable for the smaller farmer, we made hay the old-fashioned way.

First we had to mow the alfalfa, timothy or clover. I liked the alfalfa and timothy better than clover. The horses and cows didn't agree with me, however. Clover is sweeter. Unfortunately, it can sometimes cause bleeding. It also makes the animals lose their appetite for the other hay which is better for them. I didn't like clover because when it was dry it was very rough on my hands, so I wore gloves when handling it.

During the mowing I walked in front of the mower to flush out the birds and rabbits living in the hay fields so they wouldn't have their legs cut off. Snakes that were frequent in the fields could fend for themselves as far as I was concerned.

After mowing, the hay was raked into rows and loaded from the ground onto horse-drawn wagons. My job was to load the hay which had been passed up to me on the wagon so as to spread the weight evenly and balance the load. It was a dusty, sticky (particularly with clover) job, but I was a good spreader. Occasionally a snake arrived in a pitchfork clump of hay. It was my pleasure to throw that snake back to the men on the ground to do something with it. Most were non-poisonous blue racers and garter snakes but that didn't make me like them anymore than the little copperhead that had killed the kitten. I think the men on the ground sometimes passed the snakes up just to hear my

scream, so I tried not to show any fear. I didn't want to give them the pleasure.

When the wagon was fully loaded we would take it to the barn. I drove the horses slowly, avoiding changes in ground slope as much as possible so the load wouldn't slip. During hay season, slipped loads could be seen frequently on the roads. Not mine, of course!

At the barn, giant hayforks attached to ropes long enough to pull the forks to the loft picked up large clumps of hay and dumped them in the loft where they had to be spread and tromped.

Thank goodness for the hay bailer that Dad eventually bought. The bales were too heavy for me to lift and my hay-making days were over.

✳ ✳ ✳ ✳ ✳ ✳ ✳ ✳

Threshing was a memorable event in late summer and early fall. It was big-time work for men and women and dangerous. My role was basically to carry lemonade to the men and help with the large dinners that had to be prepared for up to twelve or fifteen men.

The arrival of the big threshing machine down our lane was an exciting event. "Here they come, Mom. I'm going to go open the gate to the barn lot." I rushed out the door. The men yelled, "Hi! Are you going to help us, Doc?"

I nodded yes and ran in front of them as the big machine moved to its position, leaving room for the wagons bringing the grain to be threshed alongside the thresher.

Threshing was a cooperative effort by the farmers in the area. The huge, expensive machines were bought by a group, and all of the farmers could take turns. They traveled from farm to farm helping their neighbors; in return they got their own threshing done. Threshing time had a festive air to it, though it was truly hard work for man and machine.

The threshing machines were made of four smaller machines: the thresher, the separator, the winnowing machine and the stacker. The bundles of grain were thrown onto the belt and carried to the thresher part of the machine. It was made up of rows of metal teeth. As the grain passed through, the teeth rubbed the grain from the stalks. The grain and stalks then passed into the separator, a large screen letting the grain pass through it but not the stalks. The grain then went into the winnowing machine where the chaff was blown out by blasts of air. The clean grain dropped into a weighing machine and the stalks were carried on a belt to the stacker.

I was amazed when our combine arrived after Dad bought the Hendricks' farm. The new combine did the work of both harvesting and separating the grain from the stalks. It left the straw on the ground to be picked up later.

The threshing and, later, the combine crews always loved to come to our farm because of the eats. Mom was known as the best cook in the area. That reputation made her try even harder. Mrs. Alexander and I did the serving as Mom loaded the dishes in the kitchen. At threshing time, she had every pot and pan in use, as well as her double oven and two stand-alone ovens. Fried chicken, roast beef, roast pork, mashed potatoes with chicken gravy, corn, baked apples, homemade bread and rolls, coleslaw and squash were all on the menu as were several pies and cakes. Mr. Alexander told us that the other ladies on the circuit couldn't match Mom's dinners so they didn't even try.

I rode Ginger practically all day carrying drinks to the men and messages to the ones in the fields when the threshing team was ready for another wagon.

I was always sorry to see them move on.

Dear Diary:

Farm life has been great this year. Lots of fun but hard work, too. Occasionally, I think I should forget about being a doctor and just be a farmer. But something won't let me change my mind. Maybe it's Dad. He keeps saying that medicine is his work and his hobby. Must be nice to enjoy what you do all of your life so completely. Maybe all of those years spent to become a doctor are worth it. Still when I watch him, more tired all the time these days, I wonder. Mom seems to worry about him too.

FALL

Chapter Five

Fall was the time to harvest the crops that were so diligently planted, cultivated and anxiously watched over the summer. Too much rain? Too little rain? My back-to-school classmates said that all I could talk about was the weather. To me, it was a pretty important subject. Must be—that's all I heard about at the oak kitchen table. Mom's favorite statement was, "Crops do better during dry weather than they do during floods when they all drown." Nevertheless, Gramp suggested we do a rain dance when things got too dry. Mr. Alexander, remembering his American Indian heritage, always agreed. Much to my amusement and Twylah's, he would mimic a rain dance in the barn.

Late fall was corn and potato harvest time.

Before our modernization, the corn was cut by hand using a sickle. The stalks with the corn still on them were put upright into shocks to dry. Then around Halloween the corn was removed from the stalk with machete-type knives and the husks removed. The workers wore gloves with a hook-like claw to strip the husks off the cobs.

The corn was then picked up and the ears put in a basket to put on the wagon to go to the corncrib. Gramp sometimes hired boys from my school's Boy Scout troop to help. Then Mom would have a cookout for them before they went home. It was great fun. Probably more fun than work.

Corn harvesting by these methods was dangerous work. There were too many opportunities to cut your legs and hands, with all of the sharp tools involved. Dad was always worried about really serious injuries, so his first major modernization purchase, after a tractor, was a corn picker. This equipment picked two rows of corn at a time, husked the ears which were then collected and stored in the corncrib. The stalks were used for silage as fodder for winter feeding.

Potato harvesting was more fun than work. We took bets as to who would get the plant with the most potatoes on it. The usual number was two or three. Not too often there were four or five. Wide-spaced, pitch-fork-like implements with wide prongs were used to dig into the ground and pull up the potatoes which were then stored in a bin in the basement for winter use.

❋ ❋ ❋ ❋ ❋ ❋ ❋ ❋

Fall also was the time for big time horse racing to begin. Gramp told me it was time for Peter to join his horse world.

I cried when Gramp loaded Peter into the van for the driver to take him to New York to begin his racing career. Peter and I had become good friends with the instructions given to me from Gramp on how to build trust. Standing on tiptoe, I put my arm over his neck and said, "Be a good boy, Peter, and make us proud. We love you."

Peter flicked his ears and walked, unafraid, up the ramp into the van. His eyes were bright and his coat glossy. He was in good health and seemed to be looking forward to more fun.

Gramp, Hank and I walked back to the barn without saying a word. A part of all of our lives just left. Gramp, sensing our feelings, said, "Don't worry, he'll be back every so often for rest and relaxation. Being at the track all of the time and the stress of racing requires that they let down sometimes—just like human athletes. Let's not be sad. Let's head for the pasture to check out the new babies to guess which one will be our next superstar. Hank, would you lead some of them past us so we can check conformation and spirit?"

Sure enough, there were some outstanding candidates for future champions. My sadness over sending Peter to his new life was somewhat eased by the prospects.

Dear Diary:

I miss Peter already. Mr. Alexander told me how symbolic the horse is to the Native American. Mr. Alexander made me think about the choices I would be required to make as I evolved toward being a good doctor and his certainty that I would make the right choices. I hope, dear Diary, that we made the right choice for Peter. His destiny is to be a great race horse. Was it his choice or ours?

❦ WINTER ❧

Chapter Six

Winter is the time for nature to rest. The fields are bare, just waiting for snow to come and, as it melts, to seep into the ground, providing a source of water for deep-rooted plants to use during dry spells the following spring and summer. The skies may be gray and the farm world colorless, but depressed spirits are rare in farmers. They still have the animals to care for, repairs to be made on fences, equipment and buildings and catalogs to search for the plants and seeds needed for spring planting. The record books need to be updated—which cow had which calf, which ewe had which lamb, dates of birth, and their registration papers filled out. If we were going to sell purebred stock, they had to be registered with full lineage and age validation. Each lamb and calf had a number tag in one ear. Mom did most of that. Gramp did the horse registration and spent considerable time at horse sales and reading horse journals, so he could keep up on the hot bloodlines and prices.

Gramp's office next to his bedroom was full of stacks of horse journals. When I got home from school, I'd head for his office to find out if any of Peter's or Emma's relatives had won any stake races. A stake race win upgraded a horse's pedigree and value as a broodmare or stallion. Gramp was full of stories about horses he had owned and raced and sold in the days before I came along. All horse people remember the "almost champion horses" they had owned or raised or sold before they became champions.

One winter evening, not long before Christmas as we sat around the kitchen table, the subject of horses came up as it usually did. Mom said it was "bad blood" meaning that the horse business (she called it "horsing-around") was only a different kind of gambling obsession. She didn't object, though, when one day Gramp came in from the track and threw a large roll of hundred dollar bills in her lap.

"There, Lydia, buy yourself a present. I sold one of Peter's brothers."

Mom smiled slightly. "I don't want anything, Lou. Buy some savings bonds for your old age. Don't buy another horse!"

"Don't you want to go to Florida or somewhere warm and bright? I'm already in my old age."

Mom replied, "No. I don't want to go anywhere. We have to stay here with Tootsie," slipping into Gramp's name for me. She usually called me Steph or, when annoyed with me, Stephanie.

I piped up. "Mr. and Mrs. Alexander can take care of me, Mom."

"Nonsense. They'd let you get away with too much."

I put on my coat saying, "I've got to go milk Nanny. We've got to find some way to get her to allow someone else to milk her. Some of the kids at school back off when I come too close. I think I must smell like goat."

"Tell them you don't like their cologne either. Let them think about that."

"Oh, Mom, you're so funny. I'll be back to help with supper."

Heading to the barn to milk Nanny, I stopped at the doghouse to get Brownie—a real champion rat terrier. The farmers around our area occasionally got together with their dogs to see how many rats one dog could control at a time. The farmers would bang on dishpans to get the rats out in the open from the corncribs or barns and tell the terriers to "Go get 'em." Brownie always won. He would catch one rat and pull it back so it couldn't escape while he caught another one which was just about ready to go through the hole it had come out of. Brownie would pull that one back, see another one about ready to get back in a hole and pull him back. Then he'd return to the first and second ones and keep them out in the open. He had been known to keep five rats at a time in motion.

Brownie could also climb ladders if he wanted to go to the

haymows or the upper levels of the chicken barns to look for varmints, or sometimes, just to visit me.

I often took him with me when I went to the barn particularly when it was dark. Sometimes the barn cats—just being friendly, I guess—would jump on my shoulder. I would scream thinking it was a rat. Brownie was always right there, just in case. He could also handle bats if they flew too low.

Nanny saw me coming and bleated a greeting. I was a little later than usual and her bag was full and she was getting uncomfortable. She got up on the little stand Mr. Alexander had made for her so I could sit on a stool to milk her rather than sit on the ground. Brownie cruised around checking out the place first and then lay down beside me.

The other animals were quietly eating and their body heat kept the barn a comfortable temperature except in the very coldest days of winter. In that case, we hung up heat lamps in the aisles, making sure there was no straw or other bedding that could catch fire from the lamp heat. It was my job to check on them.

There were no distractions. Just quiet time with the animal family. The animal-to-human link was close. I often wondered what they were thinking—probably the same thing I was—how peaceful the world was. Quiet, comfortable and without strife. I often sang to Nanny. I was alone but certainly not lonely.

I took back part of Nanny's milk to the house for Mom to pasteurize. Goats' milk is richer than cows' milk and easier to digest. It contains more fat and protein. Goats' milk was thought to help all kinds of health problems. Mom had regular customers for Nanny's milk. The rest we used for the puppies and the hogs.

On the way back to the house, I stopped and gathered eggs. The hens were usually dozing in the evening and wouldn't object too much when I reached under them to get the eggs. Occasionally, I'd get pecked on my hand but not too often. I'd leave a glass egg in each nest. I never understood why but Gramp told me that it encouraged them to keep laying eggs. He probably knew. Winter was not a big time egg-laying season, but I checked anyway, just in case.

✳ ✳ ✳ ✳ ✳ ✳ ✳ ✳

Winter was a family time with Thanksgiving and Christmas holidays—the time relatives from both sides of the family congregated at

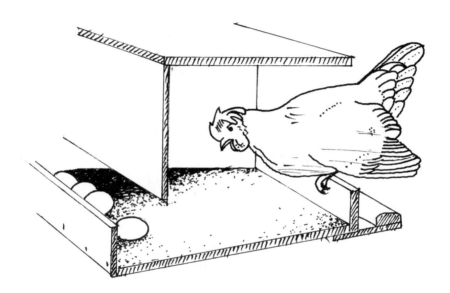

the farm with its big recreation room over the garage. All aunts, uncles, cousins and their spouses and children were invited. And, of course, they came for Mom's unparalleled dinners. The tables groaned with turkey, duck, roast beef, venison, dressing, reconstituted dry corn, kraut, turnips, squash, homemade pecan rolls, pumpkin and sugar pies. The dessert everyone waited for was the old English suet pudding with hard sauce, a family recipe from years ago, probably from one of those old-time doctors long ago.

Most of the men dozed in front of the fireplace after dinner, the kids played games like darts, monopoly or checkers. The rest of us cleaned up the mess. I don't know how Mom survived. I was certainly tired but happily so.

When it was time for the guests to leave, they all carried packages of leftovers with them, probably enough to last for a day or two.

This happened twice a year. The memories lasted forever.

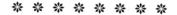

Winter was learning time for me at school, of course, but also at home. We had a complete set of Compton's encyclopedias and a set of the World Book. Unlike summer, spring and fall Mom would let me read without objecting too much that I was wasting time. She was reading, too, and working on her cookbooks saying, "So you will know how to catch a husband," with a rare twinkle in her eye.

We also played cards in the evenings. The gin rummy and euchre games sometimes got pretty rowdy. We were a very competitive family, but Gramp always reminded us not to be sore losers. Mom's philosophy, however, was different. She countered Gramp with, "Show me a good loser and I'll show you a loser." That debate was a repetitive one. Mom was not a good loser. Dad really wasn't either but then he hardly ever lost.

I worried about the horses, particularly when it was cold and snowing, but I didn't need to. They loved winter. Twylah would run around her mother, scooping up snow in her mouth when it was deep enough. Her mother, Ginger, looked on indulgently, seemingly enjoying Twylah's antics. I often had a hard time getting the two of them to come in the barn at night. Showing them a bucket of oats usually worked. Their stalls were clean and the floor soft with fresh bedding. At least I felt better. They probably longed for the summer when they could stay out all night.

In mid-January on the farm, Dad bought the adjoining farm from the family of the owner, now deceased. Some said the farmer had died of loneliness after his wife died. He had become too ill to carry out his farm chores and had sold his livestock—his companions. The farm equipment went with the land. Dad was saved any explanations of why we modernized. "Shame to waste all of that equipment," he explained. We now had doubled the size of our farm and had a tractor, a hay bailer, a a tractor, a hay bailer, a forklift, a large equipment storage shed, corn picker, gang plow—all sorts of fancy stuff.

But it wasn't going to be as much fun. My help wouldn't be required as much. Of course, I still had the animals to care for, and the quiet of the barn at night inspired thoughts of the importance of peace on earth, self-reliance and self-confidence. Ginger, Twylah, Bell, Dolly, Nanny and old Jerse, the milk cow, were all my charges. They counted on me and I accepted responsibility for them. It worried Mom. She thought spending so much time alone and with animals made me too independent and uncomfortable with people. But I didn't care about interacting with other kids. I was happy. I could be social if I wanted to, but I didn't want to most of the time.

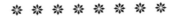

Winter was also increased medical learning time. When Dad picked me up after school, his greeting was the usual, "Hi, Tootsie, what did you learn today?"

If I said, "Oh, not much," he would say, "Guess I'll have to bring you back again tomorrow." If I said, "Oh, I learned a lot," he would say, "Guess I'll bring you back tomorrow since you're learning so much." I couldn't win.

House calls with Dad were more frequent in the winter. He didn't want me to wait inside the darkened schoolhouse so he would pick me up before his house calls. We played games on the way. He would tell me the symptoms and past history of the patients he was going to see, and I would make a provisional diagnosis. If it was different than his he would say, "We'll see." He would tell me later.

I learned about whooping cough, sore throats and sometimes their relationship to heart disease down the road, gout, and fevers of unknown origin, influenza and other conditions. The numerous causes for fainting was also a big one. On some occasions, we followed the patients to the hospital, or even took them, if Dad thought the cause of the abdominal pain was appendicitis, a gallbladder attack, kidney stones, or other potentially serious conditions that would be lethal if untreated. I would wait in the lobby of the hospital, and the nurses there would make sure I was okay. Sometimes I would curl up on the couch and sleep.

On one trip I asked, "Dad, you know all that stuff I've been reading about on the lives of famous doctors? Many of them grew up on farms. Why is that?"

Dad looked at me curiously, "What made you recognize that pattern?"

"Probably from the story Gramp told Peter and me about our family background, farmers and doctors."

Dad laughed. "I doubt that Peter remembers all of that."

"Well, he's pretty smart," I said impatiently. "Why do you think being raised on a farm is a good background for doctoring?"

Dad was thoughtful. "Well, I don't know for sure but it could be that the farm gives the opportunity to see, over and over again, the condensed version of life and death in the animals, their pain, the importance of prevention and cleanliness. Our Native American predecessors on these very lands where we are now believed that animals, indeed all living things, could teach us a lot. We just need to open our minds and hearts. You've had the opportunity to observe life in all of its phases and to perfect the art of observation. You should be able to use reasoning to know the true from the false. You probably already know more than what some young doctors need to learn by experience."

One occasion that winter had a funny ending. A man's wife called Dad because her husband didn't seem to be "with it." As the story unfurled, Dad found out that the man had been kicked in the head by a mule several days before. Dad thought the most likely diagnosis was that he had a blood clot pressing on his brain where he was kicked and we took him to the hospital in our car. Sure enough that was the case. When the clot was eliminated the man was back to normal in just a few days.

But the perfect days couldn't last.

One very cold and snowy night Dad's face was sad and worried when he picked me up. "Tootsie, your grandfather is bleeding after what should have been a minor surgery and I've got to go see his surgeon. The nurses tell me that nothing is being done."

"What are you going to do, Dad?"

"I'm going to operate and pack the bleeding site regardless of what his surgeon says."

Dr. Gibson, the surgeon, met us in the lobby. He put his arm over Dad's shoulder saying, "Ben, your dad is bleeding badly. I'm sorry but I don't think we can do anything."

Dad didn't say a word. He just plunged through the door, raced to the Intensive Care unit where Gramp lay, eyes closed, very pale and with a rapid heart rate.

"Take him to surgery, STAT and set up for an exploratory laparotomy. Call the anesthesiologist immediately." He helped the orderly move Gramp's bed and all to the surgical suite.

I watched from the hallway. When they disappeared into the surgery suite, I called Mom to let her know what was going on.

Mom was stunned. "Oh, my God! I was afraid of something like that. Your Gramp doesn't take care of himself. I'm glad your father is on the case now. Everything will be all right."

And it was. Two hours later when Gramp was back in Intensive Care they let me in to see him. I was crying.

"Don't cry, Tootsie. I'm okay. But even if I should die, I'll be in heaven with your grandmother. Just remember what I'm saying now. If I die I'm leaving White Horse, my Indian spirit guide, to watch over you. He's been good to me and he'll take care of you. Right now he's kind of busy." With that he went to sleep.

Gramp was home two weeks later, slimmer and moving slowly but regaining strength every day. Mom was cooking his favorite foods and, as he put it, he was, "Eating like a horse."

Dear Diary:

Once again Mr. Alexander told me about Native American beliefs. When I asked him about what Gramp had said about seeing Grandma again and about White Horse, Mr. Alexander took me to his cottage and pulled up a chair in front of the fireplace with its gently burning hickory log. He told me of the Indian belief in a total partnership with the world of spirits and that there were no living and dead, just a change in phases of existence. It was pretty strong stuff but somehow comforting.

I asked him what he thought about Gramp's Indian spirit guide White Horse. Did everybody have one? His answer was, "That's up to each individual. You'll learn about things like that when you're a real doctor, Tootsie."

I knew one thing for sure. Dad had self-confidence. He believed in himself enough to counter another doctor's opinion and, in so doing, he saved Gramp's life.

Chapter Seven

Winter had its bad side, too. The animals got restless, wanting to run and play, particularly the dogs. They formed a neighborhood "club" to explore all of the nearby farms. It was a dog pack. They chased rabbits and the occasional fox. But, unfortunately, for all concerned, sheep were the most fun for them. They would scatter a flock of sheep and then chase an individual sheep. They would kill that sheep with a deep throat bite, tearing out the arteries, and the animals would die. The dogs would get so excited they would keep going until whole flocks of sheep were killed. The farmers would find the sheep lying all over the pastures. Many farmers bought billy goats to run with the sheep. Sometimes the goats would chase off the dogs or discourage them by serving as the front line of defense by butting the dogs. But sometimes the goat himself would be a victim.

It came close to home one early January night. I heard the doorbell ring and a loud chorus of men shouting, "Doc, come out here. We want to talk to you."

My bedroom was on the second floor just above the front door. It had an attic access closet with pull down stairs just off of a dormer alcove where I had a dressing table and mirror. I could hear everything the men were saying.

"Doc, where's Gypsy? We want to see if she has any wool or blood in her mouth. The dog pack has been busy tonight killing sheep. We're tracking down the dogs that were involved and shooting them. Once a dog gets to be a sheep killer, he can't be retrained."

Gypsy was sleeping beside my bed. I woke her up and pulled her into the attic access, saying quietly, "Don't bark, Gypsy." Just to make sure she couldn't, I tied a silk scarf around her mouth like a muzzle. She tried to pull it off, but I sat with her holding her front paws down, whispering to her, "Be quiet, sweetie."

I heard Dad say, "I don't know where Gypsy is, Elmer. I haven't seen her. My father may have taken her back to the home place. He does that sometimes, particularly in the winter. He gets lonely and she keeps him company."

"Well, okay, Doc. Just remember we'll have to shoot her if she runs with the pack." And they walked away.

Now I had a problem. How was I going to explain Gypsy's presence the next morning? I wasn't supposed to let her stay in my bedroom—Mom's rule. I guessed I'd just have to bite the bullet and tell the truth.

The next morning at breakfast when Mom was busy putting pancakes and sausages on a platter Dad asked, "Where was Gypsy last night, Tootsie?"

I said bravely but softly, swallowing my fear of Mom's ire, "She was with me all night, Dad. In my bedroom."

A half smile crossed Dad's face. Nothing more was said except, "Well, on these cold nights, she can stay in the basement from now on. Just make sure she does."

It dawned on me that they didn't know that I knew about the sheep killings.

There were no more killings for a week or so when Gypsy was staying in the basement at night. It made me nervous. Was Gypsy a sheep killer or had the real killers all been shot? All of the farmers around us were bemoaning the loss of their dogs.

I overheard Dad talking to Gramp a few days later. "Dad, would you take Gypsy to the home place with you for a while?" He was telling Gramp the sheep-killing story.

"Sure. I'll be glad to take her with me. She's good company."

Soon the sheep killing started again, but Gypsy was thirty miles away staying in Gramp's house at night. It was a relief for all of us. Gypsy was not the dog pack ringleader.

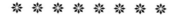

One night about that time when I was enjoying the peace and quiet of the barn, I was surprised to see Dad coming down the stairs to the animal quarters where I was sitting on Bell's back in her stall. She never seemed to mind when I'd lean forward and put my arms around her neck and my head against her mane and talk to her.

Dad sat down on a bale of hay outside Bell's stall and I went out to sit with him. "Hi, Dad. Glad to see you. Did you have a good time in the big city? Did you see a lot of old friends at your continuing education course?"

"Tootsie, I need to tell you something that pains me a great deal. I didn't go to a course. I went to University School of Medicine to see the cancer specialists."

"Cancer specialists? For Mom?" Mom had gone with him leaving me in the Alexanders' care which was unusual.

"No, Tootsie. It's me. You know I've been tired—sick too. I have a widespread cancer of the stomach, just like my mother had. I'm not going to live much longer that a month or two. It runs in families and I want you to promise me you'll get checked for it regularly when you get to be forty or so. If caught early enough, it may be curable."

"Oh, Dad," I started to cry.

"Don't cry, Tootsie. I'll be with you always."

I cried harder not able to talk.

"After I'm gone, if I can I'll let you know that I'm all right. The only sadness I see for you now is that we will need to have a sale of our animals and farm equipment. Your mom will continue to live here after I'm gone, but she can't continue to farm."

"What about Mr. Alexander? Won't he stay?"

"Unfortunately, he can't. He's going back to Oklahoma to help his brother. They still have the family farm, but it hasn't been regularly cared for. Mr. Alexander wants to restore it. He wants to make it like this one. Based on hard work, honesty and nature's bounty."

I still couldn't say anything. My thoughts were jumbled and troubled. Everything was changing. Lots of what I loved would be lost. How could this happen so quickly?

"Let's go to the house, Tootsie. Your Mom needs our company, too."

When we got the house, I asked to be excused and went to my bedroom to tell my diary about the sad news.

I heard Mom, Dad and Gramp talking for what seemed like all night.

❀ ❀ ❀ ❀ ❀ ❀ ❀

The next morning, Dad told me that they had decided that I should go to my aunt's house the day of the sale.

My response was quick and positive. "No! I want to stay and see who buys Ginger and Twylah. If I don't like their looks we can give them to the orphanage for the kids to raise and learn from them."

Dad and Mom shrugged. I knew I had won.

The next few days were busy, exhausting and unhappy ones. The barn had to be emptied and the tools arranged in the barn lot so buyers could sort through them and decide what they would like to bid on. Saddles, bridles, harnesses were in another area. Smaller items such as hammers, nails, dehorners—all maintenance items—were put in boxes so buyers could bid on the whole box. The heavy machinery, the new combine, corn picker, seeder, wagons, tractor were put around the perimeter of the sale area so buyers could walk around and inspect them without disturbing the people interested in the smaller items.

Two or three days after the official sale bills were posted, Mr. Fowler, the farmer across the road from us, knocked at the kitchen door. Mom invited him in for breakfast.

Accepting some coffee with thanks he said, "I came to talk to Doc Tootsie about Ginger and Twylah." He looked over at me.

"What about Ginger and Twylah?" Sadness was in my voice, suspecting another blow.

Mr. Fowler nodded and cleared his throat. "I'd like to buy them if it's all right with you. I have two granddaughters who are horse crazy and have been very jealous of you when they see you riding Ginger. The sale would come with the guarantee that you can visit them anytime, ride Ginger, teach Twylah the lessons she needs to be a first rate barrel racer and anything else she needs to know to live happily with her new friends. I'll build a small barn for them and their own paddock right across the road so you can see them whenever you wish. The offer includes my promise that they will never be sold."

Dad said, "Jim, that's a very kind and thoughtful offer, but we can't accept."

I broke in, "Dad! Why not?"

Dad smiled, "Just testing, Tootsie, to see your reaction. We can't sell them but we can make a gift to our good neighbor and his grandchildren, can't we?"

I got up and went over to kiss Mr. Fowler and Dad. "Thanks. Now I can go to Aunt Millie's on sale day. You wouldn't like to take Bell and Nanny, too, would you?"

Mr. Fowler smiled, "I think that can be arranged."

We all dug into Mom's pecan rolls, scrambled eggs and bacon. It made us feel better. Some things don't change.

Dad passed away in his sleep on a cold wintery night. It was an appropriate date for his memory—it was February 14, the day signifying love. Earlier that evening, he had held my hands saying, "These are strong hands. Use them well, my dear, as well as your heart." Gypsy was home again and she knew Dad was dying. She sat by his bed and licked his hand when it slipped over the side. She woke Mom up when he left us.

Farmers, physicians and their families from what seemed to be the whole country came to his funeral. He had taken care of a large number of them and, indeed, had probably saved many of their lives.

After the funeral, Mom and I were sitting at the kitchen table in the lonely house when both of us heard the bleating of a lamb. It seemed to be coming from the basement.

Startled, I said, "Mom, did we forget that we had brought a new-born lamb into the basement for his nursing lesson?"

Mom shook her head, "No. It's just your father telling us he's all right. His sense of humor. He always thought it was amusing how we mothered each baby lamb."

I didn't pursue it. It wasn't the time. I knew that Gramp like Mr. Alexander held many of the native American beliefs, but I was a little surprised that Dad believed them enough that he would send us a message. He had never wanted to hear the stories Mr. Alexander told me about the Great Spirit and that the space between life and death is so thin that the dead may influence the living. He did believe that medicine is a life-long thing and that to benefit from medicine you have to learn to relate to each other and to Mother Earth.

Mom believed now that every blinking light and creaking floor was a message. It was okay. Comforting for both her and me. The Indian message was that death is but a changed plane of living.

❋ ❋ ❋ ❋ ❋ ❋ ❋

It was during one of those quiet evenings that Mom and I shared after Dad died that I asked, "Mom, is it all right if I ask you now why we moved to the farm? You, or no one else for that matter, would ever tell me."

Mom took my hand. "I wanted you to grow up without prejudices and with values that were not those of mine or your dad's or city folks but those you learned for yourself. Dad thought we should stay closer to his practice so he wouldn't have to drive so far.

"I told him about how unhappy I was. The ladies wouldn't let me join the Women's Club; my pedigree wasn't good enough for them, even though I was married to a well-thought-of physician. I had come from a poor railroad family and didn't hold my teacup properly. Lord knows, I tried to dress appropriately, but half of the time I didn't know what they were talking about. They were a closed society. I was lonely and bored. I needed to be myself—a commoner. Finally your dad said, 'Enough is enough. Off we go.' So we moved."

I leaned over and kissed her cheek. "You'll always be someone better than they. I'll try to prove it."

"You will my dear, you will. I've convinced myself that you will be and should be a doctor. I've been wrong to try to make you like everyone else. It's all right to be different. In fact, I'm proud that you're different."

"Thanks, Mom."

The months passed. Gramp lost much of his enthusiasm for anything after Dad's death, except for his horses, that is. He told Mom and me that he had decided to live at the track near his horses. The environment should save his soul, he always said. He built an addition on to the log cabin where Hank, the groom, lived at the entrance to the stables. It was a small addition but just great for a granddaughter's visits.

Gramp called Mom every day, and I talked to him also whenever I was there. The months became years. School was taking up more and more of my time. I was editor of the school paper—a one-girl paper. I had to solicit ads, stories, editorials, sports news, club notices and calendars of events. Since I didn't have Dad to take me to school and pick me up every day, Mom and I could hardly wait until I could get a beginner's license to drive a car. Dad's Oldsmobile was a little fancy and big for me, so Gramp traded it in for me for a Chevrolet coupe. It was a great car, but then every kid loves his or her first car. The only drawback was that I had to do all of the shopping for Mom. She still wasn't a city type and hated to drive. She wasn't the best driver and I was glad not to have to ride with her anymore. All of this went in my diary and

I hid the key so Mom wouldn't be able to read what I said about her driving (or other things for that matter).

Peter Nutbert, after becoming a champion as Gramp had predicted, became a successful sire and his offspring were beginning to show some talent. His lineage would live on in the sire books.

I was nearly through my second five-year diary when Gramp called, unmistakable sadness in his voice. "Peter is sick, very sick. The vet is not certain he will make it and is considering putting him to sleep to stop his suffering."

I said, "Gramp, I'm on my way." I wanted to be with him and Peter.

When I got to the track, I couldn't believe how ill Peter looked. He was lying down and his eyes were listless and cloudy. He did recognize me, however, with a little nicker. I sat down beside him and put my arm over his shoulder and rubbed his neck gently with my other hand, talking to him about our love for each other and how everything was going to be all right. But it wasn't to be. The vet and Gramp had decided to ease his suffering and the vet put a lethal injection into his jugular vein. It was all over in just a minute or two.

When I got home that night, there was a note on my bed from Gramp.

> *Dear Tootsie,*
> *Thanks for making Peter's departure easier for him.*
> *I know he knew you were there. He sends his love as do*
> *I.*
> *Gramp*

That was the night I stopped writing in my diary. I had to start a new life. The next day I applied to a college known for its excellent pre-med curriculum. I would start in the fall.

Gramp died in his sleep two weeks after Peter was euthanized. It seemed he had no reason to keep living, according to Mom. She said it was the nicest way to die, that is, while asleep. I didn't know about that.

Gramp left another note for me, this time on his pillow. It was marked "For Doctor Tootsie."

> *Dear Tootsie,*
> *Remember what I told you the last time I nearly died but your dad saved me? I told you that I'm leaving White Horse, my Indian guide, with instructions to take care of you. He took great care of me and he will do so for you.*
> *Be good and enjoy your future. You can be just as good a doctor as your Dad. Don't let anyone, particularly the male doctors, tell you differently.*
> *Love, Gramp*

EPILOGUE

Before I signed the formal application for medical school, I wanted to see the track again, the place where I had spent such wonderful springs, summers and falls with Gramp. The urge was too strong to resist. I wanted to be absolutely sure that medicine was my future.

When I was on the country road that led to the track, a sense of peace came over me. I felt my neck and shoulder muscles relax. I almost felt like pulling over and taking a nap. But when I saw the first pond and the old icehouse, I started to get excited.

I was pleased that there wasn't too much sign of decay. The board fences were well maintained and the grass clipped. It looked like velvet.

Hank's house was just inside the gate. It had a circular drive in front although it was just a log cabin. It was just as I remembered it.

I got out of the car a bit hesitantly. This was unlike me. I was usually quite positive and in charge. But here I felt humbled. This was enduring—this farm, my background.

The doorknocker was a woodpecker. You pulled on its tail and it rapped on a piece of wood with its beak.

The door was opened by an elderly, somewhat bent over man who looked up quizzically. But before I could say anything, he said, "My word, if it isn't Doc Tootsie! Come in, Missy, come in."

I felt like a little girl again, stepping into the hallway somewhat shyly. Finally, with tears in my eyes, I hugged the old man saying over and over again, "Mister Hank, Mister Hank. I don't believe it."

"It's me, all right, young lady. Surprised I'm still alive, eh? It's this place and the horse life that does it. Best life in the world. You used to think so, too."

"I still do, Mister Hank. Tell me, who owns this place now?"

"The Bottomley Corporation owns it. Your granddaddy left enough money to keep it operational for as long as I live. I don't know for sure what's supposed to happen to it after that. Somebody mentioned an executive retreat for corporate managers. Those that like horses, that is."

"That's a good idea," I said approvingly. "Gramp was nobody's fool." Then a bit more softly, "All of his ideas were good."

"He sure loved you, Missy. Used to tell me that someday you would know more about horses than most people had forgotten 'cause you were smart and loved animals."

I was staring out the window, seeing the paddocks in the distance. I could almost see Gramp on his big chestnut gelding galloping across the pasture.

"He told me you were a nice girl, too. Never begged him for anything. Just took what came and thanked him politely for everything he did. I can still see him out trying to catch that old race mare, Emma, for you to ride. He never could. But when you'd walk out in the field, she'd come up to you to be haltered as though she could hardly wait. He'd laugh out loud and tell me, 'See there, Hank, she's got a way with horses.'"

"Mister Hank, is the apartment in the barn still livable? I'd like to stay a day or so if possible."

"Sure, Missy. Come on. We'll go back there now." He led the way and didn't say anything about my leased sports car.

As we drove back to the barn that was on the back of the farm, memories flooded me. "That's the pasture we used to keep Spinster in, and I can almost see Certain Pride racing across that hill." I pointed. Hank didn't say anything. Just smiled and nodded agreement.

When we walked into the two-story apartment that had been built at the end of the barn so the owners or their guests could stay when they came to town, my eyes were drawn to a series of mirrors lining the entranceway. "The fun house mirrors," I whispered.

"You remember? Your grandpa sent me to buy them from the carnival that came through town because you loved them so much. You used to play in front of them, giggling, saying, 'See, Gramp, and Mister Hank, I can be anything I want to be.' Your grandpa would always say, 'Course you can as long as it's being a doctor.' He loved to see you having a good time. One time my wife tried to wash the mirrors and he stopped her. Said he liked to see your little fingerprints on them. Yes, sir, I don't remember as I've ever seen a grandpa who loved his grand-daughter more."

"I haven't done much of anything yet," I said quietly and thoughtfully.

"Oh, you will, Missy. Your grandpa was never wrong about people or horses. He picked you as a winner. You're just one that takes a while to come around. Like some horses. Maybe you haven't found the right mirror yet."

I brightened a bit. "Must be some kind of record for being slow to mature. Even Man-of-War did it faster in horse years. That's seven to one human years, isn't it?"

"Something like that," Hank laughed. "You'll be all right."

"Come on, Mister Hank. Let's go look at the horses."

I was convinced that my visit to Gramp's track and seeing the fun house mirrors again had done a great deal to prepare me for my interview with the Admissions Committee of the School of Medicine. I could be anyone I wanted to be.

Provided, of course, that I got admitted to medical school at all. The number of girls in medical school had been increasing since World War II. When I had asked her why there were few women doctors, the Dean of Students said that there still was some resistance to women doctors by male physicians.

"In the sciences and medicine women have probably met the greatest test of their ability to participate equally with men," she sighed.

"Seems as though some men still think their prestige would suffer and their status in society would be jeopardized by substantial numbers of women doctors. They justify their discrimination against qualified women candidates on the grounds that women would not continue to practice after marriage. They also are concerned about whether women can totally commit themselves to medicine. Child rearing is a demanding commitment, too."

The Dean came out from behind her desk and sat in the chair next to mine. "But Stephanie, I don't worry about you. Past performance still counts and commitment still counts. Your academic record is superb. They'll have a hard time turning you down.

"I wanted to be a doctor, too," she continued, "but I guess I didn't have your stick-to-itiveness. I think society just hasn't completely outgrown the long historical patterns. Women were supposed to stay home, care for their families and do what their husbands expected of them. Women were caregivers but at the home level. There were some early role models, Madame Curie for one, but not many women doctors. The two world wars helped some because women were needed in factories and, in some military roles, they fought side by side with men. We haven't completely evolved as yet but it's coming and coming fast!

She patted my hand, "Good luck."

The interview was in a conference room in the School of Medicine's library. Five professional types sat behind a long table, their backs to the floor to ceiling windows. The chairman of the committee sat in the middle of the other four. I felt like asking them to close the blinds because the sun was in my eyes but I heard a voice telling me, "Don't be aggressive. Just smile."

Their attack started right off with the chairman asking, "Why do you want to be a doctor?"

I had been told by those who were interviewed ahead of me that this would be the first question and I had worked on a response that included words like: a noble profession, the highest calling, a family heritage, my years spent with my father making his house calls, the joy of serving, and on and on. But I didn't need to use them because the chairman didn't give me a chance.

He followed his question with, "You know that no one will marry you, don't you? You'll be smarter than any husband candidates and you'll make more money."

So there it was, I thought. If all men were like him who would want to marry any of them anyway!

After a few seconds of dead silence, I replied, "I guess I'll have to take my chances. If I can't have everything I'll choose to be a doctor. It's the only thing I've ever wanted to do with my life." I smiled at the five of them.

The chairman cleared his throat. "That will be all, Miss. We have all of your credentials here. You'll be hearing of our decision in the next week or so. Thank you for coming."

I got up and left. What else could I do? I didn't think that any further discussion with them would be useful. I thought they had already made up their minds not to admit me. Well, I'll keep trying!

It was a long two weeks but finally the letter arrived. It was a very terse letter. I had been accepted into medical school. White Horse came to mind. Did he have anything to do with it? I called Hank to tell him. His reaction was, "See? I told you that you can be anything you want to be. Don't forget to come see us at the track. There are still some champions in your future."

THE HIPPOCRATIC OATH
(IN PART)

"I swear, so far as power and discernment shall be mine, I will carry out regimens for the benefit of the sick and will keep them from harm and wrong. To none will I give a deadly drug even if solicited . . . Into whatsoever house I shall enter I will go for the benefit of the sick."

The author lived in this farmhouse as a child
and went on to become a doctor, as she dreamed.